Ice Cream and Pleasures

Pleasures

A Sandy Bay Cozy Mystery

By

Amber Crewes

Amber Crewes

ISBN: 9781653726110
Imprint: Independently Published

Other books in the Sandy Bay Series

Apple Pie and Trouble

Brownies and Dark Shadows

Cookies and Buried Secrets

Donuts and Disaster

Éclairs and Lethal Layers

A

Sandy Bay

COZY MYSTERY

Book Nine

1

IT WAS A SNOWY NIGHT in Sandy Bay, and as Meghan Truman snuggled beneath a patterned wool blanket, she felt like the luckiest girl in the world. Her new friend, Jacqueline, had invited her over for some television and girl talk while her boyfriend, Jack, had taken her out the night before to *Luciano's*, her favorite Italian restaurant in town.

"That was such a good show," Jacqueline gushed as the light from the fireplace made her eyes glow. "Let's flip over to the news; we've been watching so much of this reality show that I think my brain is turning to mush!"

"Oh, stop," Meghan protested good-naturedly. "Miss-to-Mrs. has been my favorite show since college. The contestants are so funny and ridiculous, and it's hilarious to watch them compete for one fellow's attention."

Jacqueline playfully stuck out her tongue and rose from her position on the couch. "While you watch the end of this silly show, I'm going to go grab another glass of cabernet for you. I know it's one you like, and you'll need a little wine when we switch over to a serious news show as opposed to this goofy trash TV."

Meghan chuckled as Jacqueline walked into the kitchen. "Make sure it's a small pour," she called to her. "It's my favorite drink, but I have a lot of things to do tomorrow. I'm busy at the bakery this weekend, and I have so many errands to do."

Jacqueline wrinkled her nose as she walked back into her dimly-lit living room with two glasses of red wine in her hands. "Trudy agreed to a three-day weekend? That's probably for the best for *both* of you...you did say that she's been a little moody lately."

Meghan nodded as she thought of her assistant. Trudy had been a helpful companion at the bakery for a few months, but lately, she had been fussy and irritable, and Meghan was eager to get some time away from her.

"Well anyway, here is your cabernet," Jacqueline said as she handed the glass to Meghan. "I hope you like it."

Meghan took a sip and sighed. "It's perfect," she cooed as she passed the remote to Jacqueline. "I *guess* you can change the channel now, *Jackie*."

Jacqueline laughed. "Hardly anyone calls me Jackie but I like it. It's cute."

Meghan grinned. "Jackie it is, then." She settled back against the couch and yawned. "I'm getting sleepy. I'm afraid the news will just knock me right out."

Jacqueline shrugged, but as she changed the channel

to the Sandy Bay News station, both women gasped. "Look at that," she murmured as the sight of dozens of elegantly-dressed couples filled the screen. The couples paraded around an ornate ballroom, and then the show flashed to a shot of ten smiling people being served lobster on gold plates.

"What is this? More reality television?" Meghan asked in wonder as her dark eyes widened. "This is the Sandy Bay News channel, isn't it? Surely something so fancy isn't happening in Sandy Bay?"

Jackie raised a finger to her lips. "Shhhhh," she ordered Meghan. "I want to hear what this is."

The channel cut to a shot of a young, stunningly beautiful brunette woman reporting from a studio. She had a dazzling white smile, and her eyes twinkled as she addressed the audience. "With the upcoming Governor's Ball around the corner, there is no doubt that this event will be the social event of the year in Sandy Bay. We just showed you clips from last year's event, and as a reporter *and* guest, I can say that it was a fine affair. With celebrities coming into Sandy Bay from around the world, a marvelous menu, and a live band, the Governor's Ball is a night to remember. Isn't that right, Kirsty?"

Meghan's jaw dropped. "Of course Kirsty Fisher is in charge of such a fancy event," she muttered as Kirsty Fisher, one of Sandy Bay's social butterflies, appeared next to the young brunette woman. As a business owner in Sandy Bay, Meghan had frequently interacted with Kirsty who was constantly trying to get her to help with events in town, or provide goods for a party or festival, and while Meghan admired Kirsty's commitment to her causes, she could be a bit much.

"Thank you for having me," Kirsty smiled as she flipped her blonde hair behind her narrow shoulders. "This year's ball will be the night of all nights! We have so many special guests coming to town, and of course, Governor Brown and his lovely wife, Paula, will be hosting. The tickets are five-thousand dollars per person this year, and the planning committee is delighted to see how much fun we can have. Come, everyone. Purchase tickets before they sell out!"

Meghan clapped her hands in delight. "Jackie, Paula Brown is from Texas, my home state. She was Miss Texas years ago, and then she became an actress in Hollywood. She is *so* beautiful. I grew up with a picture of her on the wall in my bedroom."

Jackie smiled. "That's adorable, Meghan. Maybe you can sneak into the Governor's Ball and meet her?"

Meghan raised an eyebrow. "I would *have* to sneak in," she admitted. "I cannot afford a five-thousand dollar ticket to the ball. Maybe someday…."

The television screen turned to black, and then it revealed a middle-aged man in a white chef's hat. "Look at that, Meghan," Jackie said as she pointed to the screen. "It's Claude Boucher. He's that famous chef from Paris. He *must* be in town as a celebrity guest at the ball."

"I *know* who Claude Boucher is," Meghan boasted. "I *do* own a bakery. Claude Boucher is one of the most famous chefs and bakers in the world right now."

The two women watched as Claude sat across from a red-headed reporter on a green leather couch. "Mr. Boucher," the reporter asked. "You will be a guest at the ball this year, but a little bird tells me that you are assisting the planning committee in designing the menu? What can you tell us about this?"

Claude leaned back and brushed the silver hair from his forehead. He smiled, and Meghan noticed the deep dimples in his cheeks. "Well, it is an honor to design the menu," Claude declared as he crossed his right leg over his left leg. "And unlike other years, we are not going to be exclusively importing the foods from France."

The red-headed reporter leaned in. "Oh? So this year will be different? Where will the foods be found for the Governor's Ball?"

Claude gestured at the camera. "From here, of course. We are celebrating local foods this year to give the Governor's Ball just a little something special. For example, we usually fly in our crème brulee from Paris, but this year, we have been investigating local options from the Pacific Northwest."

Meghan's heart began pounding in her chest. "Jackie," she whispered as Claude flashed a radiant smile to the red-headed reporter. "Jackie, they're asking *local* chefs and bakers to cater the Governor's

Ball. *I'm* a local baker!"

Jackie jerked her chin at the television. "Be quiet. We need details, lady."

As Meghan shut her mouth, Claude grinned. "We've been quietly searching up and down the West Coast for the best of *all* dining options, and I am thrilled to say that for this year, we have chosen the Truly Sweet bakery in Sandy Bay to provide the desserts for the Governor's Ball."

Meghan fell off of the couch. "Jackie," she murmured with a shaking voice. "Jackie, he just said Truly Sweet. He just announced that *my* bakery is going to be providing the desserts for the biggest event of the year."

Jackie ran over to Meghan and wrapped her arms around her. "This is fantastic news. I cannot believe this. You should be so proud."

As the two women embraced, Meghan's heart fluttered with joy. She closed her eyes and imagined her night at the Governor's Ball. She had been to fine events before, but never something as prestigious as this one. As Jackie began to squeal in celebration, Meghan felt a happy tear roll down her cheek.

"This is just truly sweet, Jackie," Meghan exclaimed as she wiped the tear from her dark eyes. "This news is truly sweet!"

2

"PAMELA, YOU ARE DOING A WONDERFUL JOB," Meghan gushed as she watched her newest employee drizzle hazelnut icing atop a freshly baked tart. "You have caught on to Truly Sweet's treat-making processes so quickly. I am *quite* impressed."

Pamela beamed at Meghan, her braces shining in the light of the sunny afternoon. Meghan had hired the teenager the previous week to do some cleaning in the evenings, but after Meghan had caught her frosting a cake like an expert, she knew that Pamela had talent and should be promoted.

"The way you fluffed the dough earlier was lovely, and I saw that you added three cups of butter to the mix. I usually only add one and a half cups of butter, but after trying your batch of tarts, I think I need to add more."

Pamela's brown eyes glittered. "I've been practicing, Meghan. Making these tarts for you was so much fun, and I just want to keep baking and baking and baking."

Trudy stormed into the kitchen, her greying hair

messy and her clothes covered in flour. "Meghan, the dishes are done and the cookies have been baked. May I go, now?"

Meghan nodded. "Sure, Trudy," she said as Trudy walked to the door. "No problem."

Pamela turned to look at Meghan. "What's her problem? I feel like she doesn't like me."

Meghan shook her head. "It's not you," she assured her as she ran a hand through her long, dark hair. "Trudy's been in a weird funk lately. Don't take it personally."

Pamela smiled. "That's what my soccer coach says when the other team is rude. It isn't wise to take things personally from people who do not know us personally."

Meghan grinned. "You are wise for an eighteen-year old," she told her. "It's nice having you around. You remind me a bit of Lori, one of the girls who used to help me here."

Before Pamela could respond, the yellow door of the bakery flew open, sending the little bells attached to the door flying about. Claude Boucher strutted into the bakery, and Meghan nearly dropped the long, plastic tube she was using to ice the tarts. "Bonjour," Claude called out as he smiled at Meghan and Pamela. "I hope I am not interrupting anything important."

Meghan's mouth was agape, and she could not form a coherent thought. She remembered Claude's appearance on the news the previous week, and the announcement that her bakery had been chosen to provide the treats for the ball, but after hearing nothing, she had forgotten about the excitement. Now, as Claude stood before her in her bakery, Meghan's face grew red, and her hands began to shake.

"We're just finishing these tarts," Pamela informed Claude as she handed him one. "Would you like to try one? I modified the recipe, but Meghan says they are some of the best she has ever had."

Claude looked from Pamela to Meghan. "I would love to sample one of the tarts, but first, I must know: who is the owner of this quaint little bakery? Where can I find the proprietor?"

Meghan stuttered, unable to maintain her composure around the famous chef. "'It's….it's….it's….'"

"It's her," Pamela said matter-of-factly as she pointed to Meghan. "She owns the bakery. I just started helping out last week."

Claude reached for Meghan's right hand and drew it to his lips. A chill ran down Meghan's spine as he kissed her hand, and she could feel her cheeks growing warm. "Meghan Truman, it is truly a pleasure to make your acquaintance. No one told me how lovely you would be, and I am so happy to finally meet you."

Meghan stared at Claude.
"Nice….nice….nice….to…nice to…."

Pamela looked confusedly at Meghan, and then she took Claude's hand. "Meghan is happy to meet you, and so I am. You have an accent. Where are you from?"

Claude graciously smiled at Pamela. "I am from Paris. I am a chef there, young lady, and from the looks of things, you are a little chef as well."

Pamela grinned. "I help Meghan here with odds and ends, but I hope to be doing more baking in the future. For now, though, I am late for soccer practice. Meghan, I'll see you tomorrow."

Meghan stared as Pamela tore off her soiled apron and dashed out of the front door. Claude returned his attention to Meghan and grinned. "Meghan Truman, I have some very exciting news for you. Have you heard of the Governor's Ball? It is the premiere event in the Pacific Northwest."

Meghan nodded, still struggling to speak, but Claude continued, "this year, we are sourcing our catering from local vendors," he explained to her. "We have searched near and far, and the planning committee has decided that your bakery will be providing desserts for the event, if you are open to the idea. Kirsty Fisher spoke very highly of you, and after reading the excellent reviews you have received after only months of your business being open, we cannot pass up the opportunity to work with you. What do you say? Will you provide the desserts for the ball, Meghan? Oh, say yes!"

Meghan nodded enthusiastically. "Yes," she told Claude, thankful that she at least could manage to answer the most important question she had been asked in her professional career. "Yes."

"Very good," Claude declared as he snatched her hand and planted another kiss on it. "With that, I must go. I will be in touch regarding the event. Take care, Meghan."

Before she could process Claude's visit and her good fortune, her tall, handsome boyfriend, Jack, burst into the bakery waving two pieces of paper in the air. "Meghan, I did it," he shouted in delight as he sprinted to where Meghan stood in the middle of the dining room. "Hey, I did it!"

Meghan shook her head, her mind still clouded with the impact of Claude's visit. "What? Jack, what are you talking about? What did you do?"

Jack's blue eyes danced with excitement, and he took Meghan's hands in his. "I scored two tickets to the ball, Meghan. We're going to the Governor's Ball."

Meghan raised an eyebrow. "Are you working security for the event or something?

Jack shook his head. "No, Meghan," he said as he squeezed her hands. "We're attending the event! This detective is off-duty for the ball. I just want a night of fun with my girl, and this is going to be an amazing event."

Meghan pulled her hands from Jack's. "I don't understand," she told him. "The tickets are five-thousand dollars, Jack. I know that you received that promotion a few months ago, but detectives can't afford that kind of ticket. The ball is important; all of the proceeds go to charity, but I do not want you to go into a financial hole just to make me happy."

Jack ran a hand through his blonde hair. Meghan could see he was frustrated, and she put a hand on his shoulder. "Jack? Where did you get the tickets?"

"It's fine, Meghan," he assured her. "My former colleague, Michelle, got them for me; she used to work here in town, but now she works in the capital for Governor Brown. She called me up out of the blue and offered the tickets, and how could I say no? A night of dinner and dancing with the most gorgeous girl in Sandy Bay? My answer was yes, and she sent over the tickets today."

Meghan bit her bottom lip. "Are you sure it's okay?" Meghan asked Jack as he crossed his arms across his muscular chest. "It's a pretty big favor, Jack. Those tickets cost a lot of money. Are you sure she doesn't want anything in return?"

Jack frowned. "She's a former professional colleague, Meghan," he told her as she stared into his eyes. "She's doing a nice thing for us, and I think we should *both* be appreciative."

Meghan shrugged. "Well, you can return one of the tickets; I was asked to make the desserts for the event, so I will be given a free spot at the ball."

Jack's jaw dropped. "It's official? They asked you? Meghan, that is amazing. I am so proud of you."

Jack picked Meghan up and spun her around the dining room as she giggled. "It's not a big deal," she protested as Jack kissed her on the cheek.

"It is a big deal," he argued. "We will dine and dance and indulge in your desserts at the ball. I'll send that ticket back over to Mitchelle, but I am so happy I will be able to be there to watch you shine."

Meghan nodded. "It will be a great time," she said as Jack kissed her on the forehead. "My desserts and my boyfriend at the best event this town has seen? What could go wrong?"

3

THE MORNING OF THE BALL, Meghan assembled her team in the dining room of the bakery to go over final preparations. It was only five in the morning, and while Meghan typically did not enjoy rising before the sun, today, she was giddy as she sipped her extra large caramel cappuccino.

"This is the biggest day of my career, everyone," she announced to the sleepy-eyed group. "I cannot thank you enough for volunteering to help me with the Governor's Ball."

"I'm your employee, Meghan. I didn't quite volunteer," Trudy grumbled.

Meghan ignored Trudy's insolent tone and continued, "Your help is so appreciated. You will be partnering with Claude's team to prepare our desserts at the event, and it will be the night of a lifetime. His team flew in last night from Paris, and I'm sure they will have a lot of tips and tricks we can learn."

Pamela grinned. "I can't believe we're going to work with people from Paris tonight. This is going to be the best."

"It will be," Meghan agreed. "Pamela, I have let Claude's team know that you will be assisting with the tarts; they seem to be your specialty, and I'm thrilled to see what you'll create tonight."

Pamela gave Meghan a playful salute. "Aye aye, Captain Meghan. Happy to assist where the Captain orders."

Meghan turned to Trudy. "The team knows that you are my top assistant," she explained. "As I will be seated with the other guests during the event, all questions regarding the desserts from Truly Sweet will be deferred to you."

Trudy frowned. "So while you dance the night away, I'm going to be working in the kitchen to make your treats while you get the credit?"

Meghan shook her head. "No, Trudy. This is a team effort. Truly Sweet would not be where it is today if I didn't have a wonderful group working with me, and I hope you know how grateful I am for your help."

Trudy mumbled under her breath, and Meghan stifled the urge to say something snarky. She didn't understand why her assistant had been so disgruntled lately, but she hoped Trudy would soon return to her normal, chipper self.

"Credit or no credit, I'm just happy to be here," Pamela declared as Trudy rolled her eyes.

Meghan ruffled Pamela's short blonde hair. "I love

your excitement, Pamela, and to further the excitement, I have a surprise for all of you."

Meghan disappeared into the kitchen, returning with two large purple garment bags. She gave one to Pamela and one to Trudy. "As the ball is going to be a night to remember, I thought that the Truly Sweet team deserved to look their best. Open your bags, ladies."

Pamela tore open her garment bag and began to shriek. "It's gorgeous, Meghan. Look at this outfit! I'll look like a proper chef in this. Meghan, thank you, thank you, thank you."

Meghan smiled. She had specially ordered the yellow chef smocks from her favorite online boutique; each was trimmed with lace, and Trudy and Pamela's initials were embroidered in large, elegant cursive on the left side. With bell sleeves and tiny white buttons that studded both sides of the coat, the smocks had been expensive, but with chefs and bakers flying in from France, Meghan wanted her crew to look like professionals.

"They're nice," Trudy admitted as she ran her hands over the long smock. "But we'll ruin them will the flour and sugar. Seems like a waste of good money to me."

Meghan pasted a grin on her face. "I was happy to buy them. I think you'll both look beautiful. So, Pamela? You will be helping with the tarts, and Trudy, you are essentially in charge. I'll be nearby if either of you need anything, though, so there should be no issues."

Pamela stood up to hug Meghan. "Thanks, boss," Pamela said as she embraced Meghan. "I'll be there right on time."

Trudy nodded at Meghan as she walked to the door. "See you later, Meghan."

Twelve hours later, Meghan took one last look at herself in the mirror as she applied a layer of mauve lipstick that matched the floor-length ballgown that her dear friend, Karen, had advised her to pick up from her house earlier.

"It was mine as a young woman," Karen informed Meghan as she nervously clutched the phone. "The color is fantastic, and the style is timeless. You'll be a dream in it."

"I hope you're right," Meghan sighed as she glanced over at the dress she had originally chosen. During her late morning shower, her little twin dogs, Fiesta and Siesta, had gotten sick on the dress, and by the time Meghan realized it, it was far too late to send it to the dry-cleaner. She had frantically called Karen who was away on holiday, and as per usual, she had saved the day.

The ballgown fit Meghan like a glove; the sweetheart neckline accentuated her shoulders and collarbone, and a simple diamond pendant rested just beneath her neck.

The empress waist hit Meghan's curves in all the right places; she was sometimes self-conscious about her womanly figure, but tonight, she felt like a princess as she smiled at her reflection. The color of the dress made her olive skin glow, and her long dark hair was pinned back into a sophisticated chignon.

"Wow," Meghan heard Jack say from behind her. She spun around to find him staring at her in the doorway of her bedroom.

"Jack, I didn't even hear you come in," Meghan said as she stared at her boyfriend. "You frightened me."

He walked to Meghan and kissed her softly on the lips. "You look stunning, Meghan," Jack whispered as he wrapped his arms around her waist. "That dress…that wasn't the one you first picked, was it?"

Meghan pulled back from his embrace and spun around, the ballgown's many layers ruffling loudly. "The dogs ruined my other dress," she admitted. "This was a last minute save from Karen. It was Karen's dress from when she was young. I was a little worried that it would be out of style; she is in her seventies, and fashion was different back then."

Jack shook his head. "It's perfect. I've never seen you look so lovely."

Meghan looked at Jack and gave a silly whistle. "You don't look too bad yourself, Detective Irvin," Meghan murmured as she leaned in to kiss Jack's cheek. "You're quite dapper in that tuxedo, my dear."

"Well, sweetheart, I had to look nice for my lady," Jack announced as he gave his elbow to Meghan. She slipped her arm into his, and they walked downstairs, Meghan careful not to trip on the hem of her skirts.

"I'll get the door for you," Jack told Meghan as he helped her into his car. "Let's go, Meghan."

Meghan settled into the car, eager to see what the Governor's Ball had in store her for and her bakery. "I'm so excited," she said. "Between my desserts being served, you looking so handsome, and rubbing elbows with Paula Brown, the former Miss Texas, I believe that tonight will be a fairytale."

"As do I," he replied. "It was so awesome that Michelle got the ticket for me.

Meghan bit her lip. "Yeah," she responded. "So awesome."

"Michelle is great," Jack gushed as he drove toward the Sandy Bay Event Hall. "Her job is so cool, too. Her transition from the police force to the Governor's staff was seamless, it seemed; she's risen through the ranks so easily. I hope I can do that someday. I'd love to work for the governor, and it would be so fun to work with Michelle again. She's the best."

Meghan furrowed her brow. "I bet it would," she said, irritated that on her big night, her boyfriend was singing the praises of another woman.

"What?" Jack asked as he looked over at Meghan.

"What's the matter?"

Meghan shook her head. "Nothing. It's just annoying that on the night I dress up like a movie star, the biggest night of my career, you're telling me all about another woman."

Jack laughed, but then seeing the serious look on Meghan's face, he stopped. "Are you serious? Meghan, Michelle is my friend."

Meghan shrugged. "I've never heard of her, and she got a five-thousand dollar ticket for you. That seems a little too friendly to me."

Jack narrowed his eyes at Meghan. "I wouldn't be coming to your big night if Michelle hadn't generously given me one of her free tickets," he said as Meghan turned to stare out the window. "You need to relax, Meghan. It's going to be a great night. Don't let this spoil it for you. Michelle is just a friend."

Meghan grimaced. "Whatever you say."

Jack reached over squeezed Meghan's hand. "Hey," he said. "Seriously, stop looking for reasons to be fussy. It's your big night, Meghan. Nothing is going to stand in the way of you, me, and one heck of a good time, sweetheart."

4

MEGHAN'S DARK EYES SPARKLED as she stepped out of Jack's car and onto the red carpet stretched outside of the Governor's Ball. Jack rushed around to help Meghan, and she slipped her arm through his elbow, forgetting the tense moments they had shared before arriving.

"Look at all of the paparazzi," Meghan whispered into Jack's ear as he guided her along the red carpet. "There are reporters here from major news networks. They came all the way to Sandy Bay for the ball. I can't believe this."

"Meghan Truman!"

Meghan glanced over her left shoulder to see a reporter waving at her from behind the metal barrier that separated the press from the guests. "Meghan Truman? Aren't you the owner of the bakery providing the desserts for the event?"

"Yes, she is."

Meghan gasped as Claude snuck up from behind and wrapped an arm around Meghan's waist. Claude nodded at Jack, and then grinned down at Meghan. "Beautiful Meghan Truman, it is so lovely to see you here."

"It's so nice to be here," Meghan sputtered as Claude tugged at Meghan's waist to lead her down the red carpet. Jack pulled back, letting Claude take Meghan away. "Smile and wave at the press, Meghan. Give them what they want."

Meghan laughed as Claude struck a pose and blew a kiss at one of the reporters.

"I'll catch up with you, Meghan," Jack called out as Claude and Meghan drew further away. "I'll see you inside," she replied.

Claude dropped his arm from Meghan's waist and took her hand, giving it a squeeze as they walked across the threshold and into the ballroom. "Get ready to be amazed," Claude purred into Meghan's ear. "This will be a night you will never forget."

"He's right," Meghan thought as they stepped into the ballroom and she surveyed the massive, beautifully decorated candle-lit room. "I will *never* forget this night."

Candles glittered on every surface of the room, and the tables were set with gold plates. Displays of red and white roses wound across the railing of the grand staircase in the middle of ballroom, and ten chandeliers hung from the ceiling. Meghan had never seen such finery before, and while she had seen images from previous balls on the news, the reality of the event was more than she could have ever imagined.

"Come, Meghan," Claude murmured as he adjusted his black bow tie. "I have so many people to introduce you to. Your desserts have already been quite the hit, and there are some fabulous people who want to meet you."

"That would be fantastic," Meghan said as she fluttered her eyelashes.

"Steve! Carol!" Claude called out to a middle-aged couple. "Meghan, this is Steve and his wife, Carol. They are dear friends of mine. Carol owns a talent firm in Los Angeles, and Steve recently retired from a career in hospitality."

"It's a pleasure," Meghan told the couple as she shook their hands.

"The pleasure is ours," Carol cooed. "Your desserts are wonderful; I spoiled my diet to eat some of your tarts, and it was sure worth it."

"Oh, Kenzie, dear," Claude shouted at a young, statuesque blonde woman. "Kenzie, come meet Meghan. Meghan, this is Kenzie. She is a top model in Paris, and she flew in for the event. Kenzie, Meghan is responsible for all of the amazing desserts here tonight."

Kenzie leaned forward to kiss Meghan on both

cheeks. "Your desserts are divine," she told Meghan in a thick French accent. "Tres magnifique."

Meghan glowed as Claude showed her off to his many friends. "Is there anyone else you would care to meet?" Claude asked as he beamed at Meghan. "I think I have introduced you to nearly everyone I know."

Meghan shook her head, but then she remembered the person she had been aching to meet since she was a little girl. "Actually, there is someone…."

"Oh, Meghan," Claude fretted as he looked down at his rose gold cell phone. "It appears there is a little disaster in the kitchen. I must go check on things. Excuse me."

Meghan watched as Claude scurried off. She looked around the room for her boyfriend, but when she did not see Jack, Meghan bit her bottom lip. "I could just stand here alone," Meghan thought to herself. "Or…."

Meghan gathered her skirts in her hands and took off toward the head table. She could see Kirsty Fisher laughing as she sipped a glass of champagne, and just as Meghan hoped, seated right next to Kirsty was Paula Brown.

"Just the woman I want to meet," Meghan said under her breath as she walked daintily toward the head table. "I can't wait to meet my hero."

She waited until Kirsty and Paula had finished their

conversation before she gingerly tapped Paula on the shoulder. "Excuse me? Mrs. Brown?"

Paula Brown scowled as she turned to glare at Meghan. "Can I help you?"

Meghan smiled warmly, but before she could introduce herself, Kirsty spotted her. "Meghan, hello. The desserts are excellent. I am so thrilled that you were able to help with the event. Paula, dear, Meghan here helped with the desserts tonight."

Paula looked up and down and Meghan and then turned back to face Kirsty. "That's nice, but why is she here now? Are you here to take my dessert order or something, Melanie?"

"It's Meghan," Meghan said softly as her eyes widened. "My name is Meghan."

"Whatever," Paula responded. "Melanie, Meghan, it's all the same. But seriously, I want dessert now. Can you take my order?"

Meghan was shocked by Paula's rudeness, but she dutifully nodded. "Sure. Can I bring you some tarts? That's the dessert special tonight."

Paula rolled her eyes. "Ugh, what a boring dessert," she announced. "Just bring me some ice cream."

"No problem," Meghan said as she nodded at Kirsty and Paula. Meghan's heart pounded with frustration as she walked away from the head table. Paula had been *nasty*, and Meghan was disappointed that someone she had been so excited to meet had turned out to be so unfriendly.

"Melanie?"

Meghan turned around to find a bespectacled man waving her down. "It's Meghan," she said to the man.

"My apologies, and apologies on behalf of Mrs. Brown," the man said. "I'm her personal assistant. She is a little fussy today, but I promise, she is usually a doll."

Meghan shrugged. "I'm sure," she answered. "Can I help you with something?"

The man nodded. "Yes, actually; Mrs. Brown wanted me to tell you that she wants dairy-free, vegan, sugar-free ice cream."

Meghan gritted her teeth. "Of course she does," she muttered under her breath. "I'll be back with that in a moment."

The personal assistant scurried away, and Meghan took three long deep breaths to calm herself down. "This is the Governor's Ball," she told herself as she walked along the perimeter of the dance floor in search of ice cream for Paula. "I need to enjoy the night and not let her get to me. After I fetch the ice cream, I'll find Jack, and we'll dance the night away."

Just as Meghan thought of her boyfriend, she spotted

him across the room. He looked more handsome than ever in his tuxedo, and Meghan admired the way it hugged his muscled shoulders. She smiled, feeling a warmth in her heart that spread to her cheeks, putting a bright red blush on her face. Meghan turned toward Jack, eager to surprise him, but before she could reach him, a stunningly beautiful auburn-haired woman leaned in to kiss him on the cheek. Jack laughed, and Meghan's heart dropped as he embraced the woman.

"Who could that be?" Meghan asked herself as her hands clenched into fists.

Just as Meghan neared her boyfriend, a shrill scream filled the room. All heads turned, and in the middle of the dance floor, a woman was lying on the floor.

"Help! Help! Help!"

Meghan recognized Kirsty's voice; Kirsty sounded panicked, and Meghan rushed to her side. Kirsty was hunched down and leaning over Paula Brown. Paula's eyes were rolled back in her head, and her face was ashen. Kirsty tapped on Paula's chest repeatedly, crying and shouting as Meghan took her by the shoulders.

"What is going on?" Meghan asked as she stared into Kirsty's worried face. A crowd formed around the women, and Meghan heard whispers as she looked down at Paula's still body.

"We were walking over to meet the Governor, and

before I knew it, she had collapsed."

"What's going on here?"

Meghan and Kirsty saw Jack run to them, taking off his tuxedo Jacket and leaning over Paula's body. "Kirsty, Meghan, I need the two of you to back away."

"Do you need help, Jack?" Chief Nunan asked as she walked through the crowd.

Jack shook his head. "Chief," he said slowly. "She's dead. Call for the coroner, Chief Nunan. Paula Brown has fallen down dead."

5

THE MORNING AFTER THE GOVERNOR'S
BALL, Meghan felt a dull ache in her heart as she
walked her dogs along the shoreline; she had been so
excited to experience the grandeur of the ball, and
everything had been ruined by Paula Brown's
unexpected death in the early hours of the event. As
Meghan tugged her little dogs along the pebbly
beach, she could not shake the melancholy
threatening to send tears spilling down her cheeks.

"Meghan?"

She nearly jumped out of her skin as Claude walked
up behind her. Without his fancy chef hat, he was
nearly unrecognizable in his street clothes, and the
dark, heavy bags underneath his eyes suggested that
he had not slept well.

"Claude," she said softly.

"What a small world," Claude replied as he raised an
eyebrow at her. This is a lonely little place to be, all
alone, so early in the morning."

Meghan pointed at the Pacific Ocean. "The waves

always calm me," she told him as the dark blue water crashed along the beach. "After last night, I needed some peace."

Claude stared into Meghan's eyes. "The ball was never going to go on again after last night," he declared as Meghan looked down at her feet. "The Governor's Ball is forever ruined, marked by the death of Paula Brown."

Meghan shook her head. "It is so sad," she said. "Such a tragedy."

"Indeed it was," he agreed. "So unexpected for her to pass away. It is strange, though, Meghan. I have heard that she had only been at the event for a short time, and knowing Paula personally, I know that she does not eat on days she attends events. The only food she would have had at the ball would have been the Welcome Tarts set out at the head table. The tarts that *you* happened to make…"

Meghan's body grew cold as she processed Claude's words. "What exactly are you trying to say to me?" she asked as Fiesta and Siesta skipped through the water.

Claude sighed. "I'm not saying *anything*, Meghan Truman," he haughtily replied. "But I can say that your treats had been served to Paula, and she had taken a bite of her tart. Kirsty Fisher told me that. And I can also tell you that that fact alone makes you look very, very interesting to the police, Meghan."

Meghan shook her head. "I didn't make the tarts," she argued. "My team arrived at the event hours before I did; they used my recipe, but I didn't personally make the tarts, Claude. And who is to say that the tarts had anything to do with her death?"

Claude bit his lip. "I'm not saying that. But, I did check on your team in the kitchen early in the day, and that assistant of yours? Trudy? Well, she should be called Broody Trudy; her attitude was terrible, and she lacked professionalism. Meghan. I'm just saying, if Broody Trudy had gotten angry and wanted to frame you, or wanted to do away with Paula for the fun of it, it wouldn't surprise me."

"That is *enough.*"

Jack Irvin walked up to Claude and Meghan, his own dog, Dash, barking happily at Fiesta and Siesta. "Claude, that is enough; the Sandy Bay Police Department is investigating Paula's death, and it is inappropriate of you to say such things to Meghan."

Meghan raised an eyebrow at Jack. "Hey, Jack," she said coolly. "Nice to see you here today."

Claude looked between Meghan and Jack. "I sense some trouble in paradise with you two lovebirds," he declared in his thick accent.

Jack cocked his head to the side. "Trouble?"

Claude winked at Jack. "I would be in trouble too if I had been paying attention to gorgeous auburn-haired ladies instead of my own date.

Jack's jaw dropped. "Meghan? What is he talking about?"

Meghan crossed her arms across her chest and said nothing. Claude grinned antagonistically. "She didn't say anything, but I saw this lady's date chatting with someone else last night just before Paula dropped dead. Perhaps you two have some talking to do."

Jack frowned. "Meghan, I *was* talking to another woman, but you should have come over to say hello. It was Michelle. We were catching up, and she wanted to meet you."

Meghan glared at Jack. "After I saw her kiss your cheek, I didn't think that I should interrupt your conversation," she pouted.

Jack gasped. "Meghan," he said in shock. "I told you that Michelle is one of my old friends. There's nothing between us. She gave me a friendly peck. It was nothing."

"For it being nothing, someone sounds rather defensive," Claude sneered as Meghan crossed her arms across her chest.

"Look, man," Jack said as he turned to address Claude. "This is between *us*. Besides, you were summoned down to the police station for some initial questioning; if you say one more word, I'll take you down there in handcuffs."

Claude waved a hand dismissively. "Please," he muttered. "You Americans…"

Jack puffed up his chest. "What did you say to me? Say it to my face."

Meghan stepped between the two men, nearly choking on the thick, musky scent of Claude's cologne. "Stop it," Meghan ordered as she placed a hand on Jack's chest and tried to shoo Claude away. "This is ridiculous. Claude, the police will get to the bottom of Paula's death. Stop asking me questions and making matters worse. Jack, you and I need to have a private conversation. Why don't you just go on home, and we can talk later."

Claude turned on his expensive heeled leather shoes and stormed away. Jack looked sadly at Meghan.

"Meghan…"

Meghan put a finger to his lips. "Shhhh," she demanded. "Don't talk to me right now. My night and my dreams for the evening were destroyed, and you didn't make anything better. Right now, I wouldn't mind if I never had to look at you again, Jack Irvin."

6

THAT EVENING, MEGHAN WAS DESPERATE to get out of her terrible mood. She had tried all of her usual tricks; from taking a long bubble bath, to a cozy cup of jasmine tea, to indulging in chocolate covered cherries, her favorite candy, nothing was helping to settle her spirits. She was annoyed by Claude's not-so-veiled suggestion that *she* had had something to do with Paula Brown's death, she was upset that Jack had been too preoccupied with catching up with Michelle to be by her side at the ball, and she was devastated that the event had ended not with her business gaining even more attention, but that someone had perished without warning and the Governor's Ball was now considered a tragedy.

As Meghan lay beneath her goose feather comforter, she breathed in deeply as the sound of the rain pulled her into a state of relaxation. It was a dreary evening; the air was bitterly cold, and the rain pounded upon the roof of Meghan's apartment. "I have to pull myself out of this funk," she murmured to herself as Fiesta licked her ankle. "I've wasted too much time today being grumpy; last night was not what I expected, but I need to pull it together. I know what I will do. I will march myself downstairs and work on a new recipe. I've been dreaming of experimenting with strawberry extract and fresh basil for a batch of scones, and what better time to try something new.

Ten minutes later, Meghan was happily kneading dough and singing to herself as she dreamed of a delicious new way to bake her famous scones. As she cut the tops off of the enormous, juicy red strawberries she had specially purchased from an organic farm in Mexico, she heard a knock at the door.

"Who could that be?" she wondered aloud as she walked to the yellow door and peered out of the peephole. A short, plump man looked up at her, and she opened the door. "Can I help you? We're closed tonight."

The man shrugged. "It's cold and rainy," he said, adjusting the collar of his tan trenchcoat. "Any chance you could spare a cup of coffee for a drenched stranger?"

Meghan saw that the man was covered in rain. Her heart sank as she thought of turning him away, and she stepped back to gesture him inside. "Come on in," she warmly invited the man. "I don't have any fresh coffee, but I do have some jasmine tea, my favorite."

"Perfect," the man breathed as he took a seat at one of the little white iron tables in the dining area. "I've been trying to find something that's open all night, and this town is *dead*."

"I'm not surprised," Meghan admitted as she delivered the steaming cup of tea to the man. "With what happened at the Governor's Ball that night, a lot of people in town have closed down their businesses for the next few days."

The man leaned in, raising an eyebrow and placing his hand on his chin as he listened intently. "Can you tell me more about what happened? I'm not really from here…"

Meghan sat down at the table across from the man. "Don't mind if I ramble," Meghan said as she leaned back in her seat. "It's been a tough twenty-four hours, and if you don't mind, I would love to just vent."

The man smiled. "Go on. I'm here to listen."

Meghan tucked her dark hair behind her ears and continued. "It all started when I was asked to make the desserts for the event. Then I found out that my stupid boyfriend, Jack, had gotten tickets to the ball from……"

****

"I'm glad we could do this," Jack said cautiously as Meghan sipped her caramel latte. "I know this is your favorite coffee shop, and I thought a cozy little coffee date would be the perfect place to talk things through."

It was the morning after Meghan had opened the bakery to the stranger, and after a pleading voicemail from Jack, along with a barrage of text messages and emails, Meghan had agreed to meet with him in person to discuss the Governor's Ball.

"It was really nothing, Meghan," he assured her as she crossed her left leg over her right leg and stiffened in her seat. "Michelle is just an old pal. You have to believe me."

Meghan shook her head. "It just looked like an awfully familiar moment between the pair of you," she informed her boyfriend as he sat nervously across from her. "The kiss she gave you...I didn't like it, Jack."

Jack buried his head in his hands, and Meghan saw his shoulders begin to shake. "I'm so sorry, Meghan," he whimpered. "I should have introduced the two of you before the event. I should have stayed by your side and followed closely behind when Claude whisked you away. This is all my fault."

Meghan felt the warm rush of relief; Jack knew that he had made a mistake, and he was admitting to his poor decision-making, as well as providing a satisfactory apology. Meghan could see that he was upset, and she wanted nothing more than to wrap her arms around Jack and comfort him.

"Hey, Meghan? Saw you in the paper this morning. Have you seen this?"

Meghan shook her head as Stanley, the owner of her favorite coffee shop, slapped a newspaper on the table in front of her. "Check this out, Meghan," Stanley said with a stern look in his eye.

Jack snatched the paper from Meghan and began to read the article. "Sitting in her bakery, all alone on a cold, dreary night, Meghan Truman should have been comforted by her boyfriend, local detective Jack Irvin," Jack read aloud.

"What is this?" Meghan asked. "What on Earth? Is this a satire?"

Jack continued, "Meghan Truman had a lot to say about the night of the Governor's Ball. She had a lot to say about Paula Brown, the former Miss Texas and now late wife to our beloved Governor. She had a lot to say about her bakery, and her hopes and dreams for Truly Sweet, a treasured establishment in downtown Sandy Bay. Meghan Truman also had a lot to say about her boyfriend, and his lack of good judgement on the night of the ball."

Meghan stared at Jack, her dark eyes wide as his face turned red. "Jack? I have no idea where this came from…."

Meghan reached over and grabbed the newspaper

from Jack. She glanced down at the author's name, and when she saw the author's tiny headshot in the corner of the page, she shrieked. "That was the man in the bakery last night!"

Jack stood up. "What man? Are you serious, Meghan? You got angry that I said hello to an old friend, and then you blabbed about me to some guy at your bakery?"

Meghan shook her head. "I didn't know he was a reporter," she protested as Jack turned to walk toward the door. "I thought he was a customer at Truly Sweet."

Jack stopped. "You talk about me like this to customers?" he asked as Meghan's eyes filled with tears.

"No, Jack, please understand. It was a long day, and this stranger wandered into the bakery. I didn't know he was a reporter. I started chatting with him, and after everything that happened, I just lost it and began to vent. I don't talk about you to other people, I promise."

Jack scoffed. "It sure looks like you did some damage with this article, Meghan. I am humiliated. I am leaving. We can talk about this later."

Meghan tugged on Jack's sleeve. "Jack, *please*," she begged as Jack walked to the door. "Don't leave like this; I didn't mean what I said about you. I was just angry."

Jack frowned. "I'm still humiliated. I don't want to talk about this any further in public, Meghan. I'll call you tomorrow, or maybe the next day, and we can settle things then."

Meghan began to sob as Jack left the coffee shop. Stanley, who had been watching the encounter from his station at the register, came to Meghan's side. "Meghan?"

Meghan sniffled. "Yeah, Stanley?"

Stanley grimaced. "That was a scene, Meghan, and I can't have a scene in my establishment. You're going to need to go."

Meghan's jaw dropped. "You're kicking me out?"

Stanley nodded. "Sorry, but this is a no-drama zone, Meghan. That looked like a lot of drama to me."

Meghan gathered her red purse and her latte and walked outside. She shivered as the freezing air hit her skin, and she balled her hands into fists thinking of the life she left behind in Los Angeles to move to Sandy Bay. "Los Angeles was a no-drama zone," Meghan muttered as she walked home. "I moved to this town hoping for a fresh start, expecting a small town to be sweet and pleasant, not filled with unexpected deaths, murders, and *my* reputation constantly on the line. I'm sick of all of this! If something doesn't change, I am of half a mind to pack up my things and leave Sandy Bay *for good.*

7

"THE SUN IS UNUSUALLY BRIGHT TODAY," Jacqueline complained as she adjusted her sunglasses across her ski-slope nose. "It's winter in the Pacific Northwest, and the sun is practically blinding me."

Meghan adjusted the green woolen scarf she had wound around her neck. "I'm not complaining," she told Jackie as the two women stood together in Sandy Bay Square. "It's warmer than it usually is, and if we are going to stand outside in the winter all afternoon, I would much rather the day be too sunny than too chilly."

Meghan and Jacqueline stood amongst hundreds of Sandy Bay residents for a special ceremony that had been hastily scheduled to memorialize Paula Brown. The governor himself had traveled back to Sandy Bay to dedicate a plaque in the square in honor of his late wife, and the entire town had gathered for the ceremony.

"You know, it *is* bright out here," Meghan admitted as she shielded her eyes from the bright sunshine. "It feels a little wrong to have such a somber ceremony on a beautiful day."

"I can't believe Governor Brown is out and about so soon after his wife passed away," Jacqueline whispered into Meghan's ear as Kirsty Fisher approached the platform that had been set up in the middle of the square.

"Attention, everyone," Kirsty called out in a quivering voice as she ascended the platform and stepped forward to speak into the microphone. "Good afternoon. My name is Kirsty Fisher, and I was one of Paula's closest friends."

Meghan raised an eyebrow at Jacqueline. "Were they really?"

Jacqueline shook her head. "Maybe in Kirsty's mind…you know how she likes to put on airs!"

Meghan giggled, but then silenced herself upon seeing the stern look from the couple standing next to her.

"The tragedy of Paula's death is unforgettable, but we have gathered here today to commemorate her passing with something special. The Governor has brought a special plaque to dedicate to Paula's memory. I thank you all for being here today, and I hope that we can all send our thoughts and good wishes to the governor at this time."

The Governor appeared behind Kirsty, and she kissed him on both cheeks. Meghan noticed that he looked exhausted; with dark, deep bags beneath his eyes, and red, swollen eyes, Meghan's heart ached for the governor, despite his wife's rudeness toward her at the ball.

"Thank you, Kristy," Governor Brown said as Kirsty wiped a tear from her eye with a monogrammed handkerchief.

"See?" Jackie muttered. "If his wife and *Kirsty* were truly dear friends, surely the governor would know her name…."

"Shhhhhh," Meghan hushed as the Governor continued.

"Paula had a vibrant, exciting life; she was Miss Texas, she was a film star, and most recently, she was my beloved wife and the first-lady of our state…."

"Excuse me? Meghan Truman?"

Meghan jumped as someone tapped her shoulder. She turned around and squinted; the sun was directly in her eyes, and she could hardly make out the figure in front of her. Meghan could tell it was a woman, and she held a hand in front of her face to shield it from the bright light.

"I'm with the Governor's staff," the woman explained quietly. "He would like to speak with you after the event. Take this pass and go to the VIP tent after his talk."

Meghan blinked in confusion, calling out as the woman turned and walked away, "Why does the

Governor want to talk to me?"

The woman did not answer, and Meghan turned to Jacqueline. "What was that all about?"

Jacqueline shook her head. "I have no idea," she replied. "That woman was gorgeous. I wonder what she does on the Governor's staff."

Twenty minutes later, the Governor finished his speech, and Meghan took off toward the VIP tent. She pushed through the crowd, careful as she wove through the people politely clapping for the Governor. When she reached the tent, a uniformed guard examined her pass, and then he waved her inside.

"Ahhh, Meghan Truman."

Meghan's hand flew to her mouth in shock as the Governor greeted her by name.

"Thank you for joining us here, Meghan," the Governor said graciously as he loosened his blue checkered tie and took a seat on a white folding chair. "Please, sit."

Meghan sat down on a black folding chair, and the Governor took her hand in his. "My assistants and Paula's assistants informed me that she was a bit…brisk to you at the event. My apologies, Meghan."

Meghan cocked her head to the side as she glanced around the tent. A table filled with deli meats and cheeses was on the far right side, and generators were plugged in to warm the small space.

"How do you know who I am?" Meghan asked.

The Governor chuckled. "It was my ball, remember? The ball is my favorite event each year, and I make it my business to know who is coming and going. I've actually been enjoying your desserts for months now; my assistants have an order sent over each week, and it was my idea to feature your treats at the event."

Meghan blushed. "That explains the order we send to the capital each week," she murmured. "Thank you for thinking of me. Your business means a lot to me. I'm also so sorry about your wife. She was a hero of mine when I was a child. I'm from Texas originally, and I always admired her spirit."

The Governor took Meghan's hand and gave it a squeeze. "Thank you for saying that," he said softly. "It was a shock when my wife died—the police are suggesting it was a murder, can you believe that? I am devastated, but I am so glad I got to come to Sandy Bay today to lay the plaque."

Before Meghan could respond, a young man came to the Governor's side and whispered in his ear. "Oh, excuse me, Meghan," the Governor apologized. "My assistant here says I have a conference call scheduled. I will be right back!"

As the Governor left the tent, Meghan was shocked when Jack walked inside. "Jack?" Meghan asked.

"What are you doing here?"

Jack nodded at the walkie-talkie in his hand. "You would know if you would answer my calls," he muttered. "I'm working security. I saw you come in here, and I wanted to make sure you are okay. What were you and the Governor discussing?"

Meghan tossed her dark hair behind her shoulder. "That's really not your business," she said feistily. "Your *friend*, Michelle, is on his staff. Why don't you go ask her?"

Jack narrowed his eyes at Meghan. "Don't talk like that, Meghan," he said. "Michelle is here today, but she is just a friend. In fact, she was the one who gave you the pass to come back here."

Meghan gasped. "I didn't recognize her," she replied. "The sun was so bright, and I didn't know it was your friend from the dance floor."

Jack crossed his arms across his chest. "Meghan," he began. "We have to talk about this. Michelle is just a friend, and if you can't accept that…well, I'm afraid that if you cannot get over this Michelle thing, we are really going to need to have a serious conversation about our future as a couple. I can't do this for much longer, Meghan, and if we need to break up, then let's just do it now."

8

AS MEGHAN SIPPED HER CARAMEL LATTE, her heart sank as she recounted the chaos of her evening; following her quarrel with Jack, the couple had met in the park to discuss their relationship. After two hours of fighting, Meghan and Jack had decided to remain a couple, but both parties knew that they needed some time apart. They decided to take a few days away from each other, and while Meghan was sad that she and Jack were going through a rough patch, she was happy that they had decided to stay together as a couple.

The other chaotic part of Meghan's evening took place upon Meghan's return from her lengthy conversation with Jack. As Meghan walked into the bakery, she heard Trudy screaming at Pamela from across the dining room.

"I don't care if you are talented, or pretty, or the Queen of England," Trudy snarled as Pamela cried. "I am Meghan's assistant, and when she is gone, I am in charge!"

Meghan saw Pamela's lip quiver. "I only asked if I could help with a different project, Trudy. I didn't mean to make you mad."

Before Trudy could speak, Meghan held her hands up. "What is going on in here? Trudy? What is the meaning of this?"

Trudy shook her head. "That little girl just prances around here like she owns the place."

Meghan frowned. "Pamela is a great help to us, Trudy," she argued. "And as the owner of this place, Trudy, I have concerns we need to address. Pamela? If you could take your things and head home for the night, I think Trudy and I really need to speak in private."

Pamela nodded, and she gathered her jacket and backpack. "Bye, Meghan. Bye, Trudy."

Once Pamela had closed the door, Meghan sat down at one of the little white tables. She gestured for Trudy to join her.

"I have some concerns, Trudy," Meghan informed her employee as Trudy glared at her. "Your attitude has been concerning. Can you please help me understand what is going on? You've seemed tense here, and I even received some complaints about your professionalism at the ball. I heard you were snippy with some of the guests, and I also heard that you had a camera out and were taking selfies. You know we cannot do that at an event. That is unacceptable."

Trudy's jaw dropped. "Are you serious? People are

talking about me? What the heck, Meghan? I can't believe this. All I do is work my tail off here, and you make me feel bad by saying these things?"

Meghan shook her head. "No, Trudy," she protested, placing a hand on Trudy's shoulder. "I am worried about you. You have always been happy-go-lucky, and lately, it's seemed as if something is wrong."

Trudy rose from the table. As she turned to leave, she stopped and waved a fist at Meghan. "This is ridiculous. See if I don't go join some other bakery, Meghan. I am sick of the games and nonsense."

Trudy stormed out of Truly Sweet, and Meghan forced herself to take three long, slow breaths. "Well, that was *exactly* what I wanted to deal with after a long argument with Jack," Meghan muttered sarcastically. "Ugh, I need to take a walk and clear my head."

Meghan gathered her red purse and locked up the bakery. She was happy that the air wasn't too cold, and she tucked her hair behind her ears as she wandered through the town.

"Two wrongs don't make a right," Meghan thought to herself as she walked. "And I want Trudy to be back to her normal, cheerful self. I know what I will do! I will go down to the fruit market and get a basket for her; maybe if Trudy knows how much I appreciate her, she will relax a bit. I will get the basket for her and surprise her with all of her favorites, and maybe things will go back to normal."

Meghan smiled to herself as she imagined the happy look on Trudy's face when she surprised her with the fruit basket. She set off toward the fruit market, eager to make things right with her assistant. As Meghan perused the aisles of fresh fruit, she noticed a familiar-looking man staring at her from across the market. "That's odd," Meghan thought as she studied the man's face. "Where have I seen him before?"

Suddenly, Meghan remembered why she recognized him; the man was Paula Brown's personal assistant. They had spoken briefly at the Governor's Ball. Knowing that the man was probably mourning his late employer, Meghan decided she needed to give her condolences. She put the fruit back in its bin and made her way over to the man.

"Hey," Meghan said softly. "Do you remember me? I'm Meghan. You are Paula Brown's assistant, yes?"

The man looked down at his shoes. "I *was* her assistant," he gently corrected. "Rest in peace, poor Paula."

Meghan touched his arm. "I'm so sorry for your loss. Paula must have been such an interesting woman to work for. What was your name?"

"I'm Donnie," the man said. "Meghan, I'm glad you said hello."

Meghan nodded. "Of course," she said. "How are you doing? What a difficult time it must be for you."

Donnie shrugged. "It hasn't been easy," he admitted. "But Governor Brown is a good guy; he's offered to find me another spot within his own staff, and I am so thankful to be employed by the Browns."

Meghan smiled. "He seemed like a kind man."

Donnie agreed. "He is the best," Donnie told Meghan. "I have learned so much from the Browns. I want to get into politics myself someday, and I am in such a better position now that I've had

so much exposure to the way they do things. It isn't easy; the Governor demands excellence, as did Paula, but I can only thank them for the experiences I've gained."

Meghan placed a hand on her heart. "That is a wonderful thing to say about your employer," she gushed. "I can only hope my employees feel that way about me."

Donnie smiled. "I'm sure they do. You seem like a nice gal. Anyway, I need to run, but I have to tell you that your treats were fantastic. I loved your tarts at the event, and I've been craving more."

Meghan reached into her purse and fetched a Truly Sweet giftcard. "Here," she said as she pressed the card into Donnie's hands. "Take this. Swing by any time for a treat; it's *my* treat!"

Donnie grinned. "You are adorable. I will have to talk to the Governor to see if we can do a mass order of your treats for his mansion and offices. I know you already do a shipment to him each week, but I think a mass order would be better for all involved."

She clapped her hands in excitement. "You would do that for me? You just met me, Donnie."

He winked at Meghan. "You seem truly sweet, Meghan," he cooed. "What kind of future politician would I be if I didn't extend a hand out to the little people every once and awhile?"

9

"THAT LOOKS SO GOOD on you, Meghan!" Jacqueline gushed as Meghan showed off a chunky knit sweater. "Olive is definitely your color; it makes your skin just *glow*! That would make for such a cute outfit for New Year's Eve."

Meghan spun around in the dressing room of Smitten Kitten, the women's boutique around the corner from Truly Sweet. Jackie had suggested a little shopping date to get Meghan's mind off of Jack, and Meghan had gladly taken her up on the invitation.

"Are you sure it isn't too flashy?" Meghan asked as she stared at the sweater's square neckline. "These puffy sleeves feel a little too high fashion for plain old me."

Jacqueline smacked Meghan playfully on the bottom. "Meghan, you are beautiful. Your thick, dark hair is the envy of every girl in Sandy Bay, your dark eyes have that sparkle to them, and your smile brightens every room you walk into. That sweater fits your body perfectly, Meghan, and I would be a bad friend if I didn't let you buy it. Besides, it's winter now.

Surely you need a few cute new pieces for your wardrobe. This isn't warm Los Angeles, after all."

Meghan glanced back at herself in the mirror. "I think you're right," she admitted to Jacqueline. "This is a good color for me, and I do like the way this sweater fits. Okay, Jackie, you have convinced me. Add it to my pile."

"Yes!" Jacqueline said. "Hey, Meghan? Now that it's been a few days…well, I hate to ask, but what happened at the ball? I didn't want to ask too many questions, but since you seem so relaxed….and it's just us two in this dressing room. Care to share?"

Meghan sighed. "It's fine," she relented. "At the ball, Paula was a bit rude to me, and I was upset. I went looking for Jack, and I saw him getting a kiss on the cheek from some stupid girl he was friends with back in the day."

"I wondered why the pair of you were taking a few days off," Jacqueline said as she handed another sweater to Meghan to try on. "Who is the girl?"

Meghan rolled her eyes. "Jack says she is just a friend, but from the looks of it, it seemed a bit fishy; she was one of those drop dead gorgeous girls who just looks like she could sneakily steal a boyfriend from right underneath someone's nose."

Jacqueline shook her head. "That's awful," she said. "I can't believe Jack would talk to someone like that."

Meghan laughed sadly. "You know how guys are when they see a pretty face…."

Jackie watched as Meghan slipped a soft blue turtleneck over her head. "No," Jackie dismissed as she looked at Meghan's torso. "That isn't flattering. Take it off."

Meghan obeyed, removing the sweater and hanging it on the rack in the dressing room. "I think I have enough new clothes to last me a lifetime," Meghan told Jacqueline as she giggled at the pile of skirts, tops, underthings, and accessories. "Let's get out of here, Jackie; I don't think my bank account can take any more major hits!"

Jacqueline chuckled, and the two women gathered the pile of clothes. As they exited the dressing room, they ran straight into a thin, auburn-haired woman who was sitting primly in a love seat in the corner of the main dressing area. It was Michelle, Jack's friend. Meghan gasped.

"Meghan," Michelle said coolly, her hands clenched together and resting on her left knee. "Pleasure seeing you here. I can't say it was a pleasure *hearing* you, though; do you often speak ill of people behind their backs in public?"

Before Meghan could respond, Jacqueline stepped forward. "She doesn't speak ill of people who aren't trying to steal her boyfriend!"

Michelle laughed. "I'm not trying to steal anyone's

boyfriend," she informed Meghan and Jackie as she flashed her left hand at the women and dangled her ring finger in front of her face. "I'm engaged, ladies."

Meghan stared at the enormous, princess-cut diamond ring glittering on Michelle's hand, but Jacqueline continued, "why would an engaged woman buy a ticket that expensive for Meghan's boyfriend to go to the ball? That doesn't make sense, Michelle."

Michelle rolled her eyes. "You two are acting like children; those tickets were free for us working for the Governor, and after chatting with Jack and hearing him rave about his girlfriend, the famous Meghan Truman, I thought it would be a *kind* gesture to offer him a free ticket. Had I known that Jack's girlfriend would speak so poorly of me, in public, nonetheless, perhaps I would have given that ticket to my own fiance."

Meghan's body grew hot with shame. "I'm sorry," she whispered to Michelle. "I spoke too soon; it was so kind of you to get the ticket for Jack, and I shouldn't have judged you before I met you. That wasn't fair."

Michelle rose from the love seat and shook her head. "Too little, too late, Meghan," she hissed to her. "You cross me once, and you don't get the chance to cross me again."

Jackie raised an eyebrow. "What is that supposed to mean?"

Michelle smirked. "I'll be something big someday," she informed Meghan and Jackie. "Just you wait; the Governor is grooming me to take over his role someday, and sooner than later, little twerps like you two will mean nothing to me. I'll be in charge, and you two will still be pathetic little nobodies in this pathetic little town."

As Meghan stared, Michelle collected her purse and tossed her auburn hair behind her narrow shoulders. She sashayed out of the dressing area, and Meghan's eye filled with tears. "She heard me being so mean and petty," she cried as Jackie shook her head. "Michelle *hates* me, Trudy is still angry at me, and Jack and I haven't spoken in two days. What else could go wrong, Jackie?"

10

THE NEXT MORNING, Meghan was trying to hide her low spirits from Pamela as the two iced cupcakes at the bakery. Despite leaving the fruit basket at Trudy's door several days earlier, Trudy was not returning Meghan's calls, and Meghan was concerned that her relationship with her assistant was ruined. As the day went on, Meghan continued to fret, and finally, she decided it was time to call it a day.

"Pamela? I know it's early, but I'm going to close up shop; you can clock out at your scheduled time, but why don't you finish up those cupcakes and then get out of here?"

Pamela nodded. "Sure thing, Meghan. I'll wrap these up and then see you tomorrow."

Meghan began to clean the kitchen, and as she scrubbed the dough stuck between the metal ridges of her mixing spoons, she ventured deeper and deeper into her own thoughts. She barely registered the sound of Pamela leaving, and as Meghan tidied the kitchen, she pondered her predicaments.

"Maybe I could send an apology note over to

Michelle," Meghan thought as she poured soap into a wooden bowl. "I wasn't happy about her connection with Jack, but it sounds like I was the one who jumped the gun. I feel terrible that she overheard us."

Meghan pulled out a tiny bristle brush and began to scrub a set of knives. "And Trudy…if she doesn't answer my calls soon, I am just going to have to go over to her house. She has been a dear friend and a valuable employee. I can't lose her."

Meghan bit her bottom lip as she thought of her greatest worry, the issue that had been tugging at her heartstrings. "And Jack…what am I going to do about Jack? I was so angry at him, but it sounds like I may have been out of line…"

Suddenly, Meghan felt a tap on her shoulder. She reached for one of the knives, gripping it sharply in her left hand and slowly turning to face whoever was behind her. Meghan quickly held up the knife in front of her face, waving it back and forth and screaming.

"Meghan, stop screaming, it's just *me*!"

Meghan was stunned to find Jack standing before her, his blue eyes red and his blonde hair messy. She placed a hand on her racing heart and lowered the knife. "What are you doing here, Jack?"

Jack gestured toward the door. "Didn't you hear me come in? I walked right inside and shouted your name."

Meghan shook her head. "I was day-dreaming," she admitted as adrenaline filled her body. "I had no idea you were here."

Jack sighed. "Meghan, we need to talk…"

Meghan nodded emphatically. "Yes, we do. Can we sit in the dining room?"

Meghan and Jack walked into the dining room and sat across from each other at one of the little white tables. "I want to say I'm sorry," Jack began as he folded his hands atop the table. "I should have been more considerate of your feelings, Meghan. Michelle is honestly just a friend; she has a fiancé of her own who she is very much in love with, but I should have explained more to you before throwing her into the mix. I've been trying to get close to her so that maybe someday, I could get a job with the Governor."

Meghan nodded. "Jack, thank you so much for apologizing," she said to him as she reached over to take his hands in hers. "But I was the one who jumped to conclusions. I let my emotions get the best of me, and I should have taken a moment to truly listen to you and what you were telling me. I want to apologize to you, Jack. I am sorry I was nasty, I am sorry I didn't take you at your word, and I am sorry that we didn't have this conversation sooner. That day we met to talk in the park was so difficult; I was exhausted and so confused, and I wish we had been able to talk like *this*."

Jack rose from the table. He pulled Meghan up with

him, and gathered her in his arms. Jack wrapped his arms around Meghan's waist, moving her closer to him until she could feel the beating of his heart. "Meghan," Jack whispered in Meghan's ear. "Meghan, I *love* you. We have been through so much together since you moved to Sandy Bay, and I don't want to lose you."

Meghan blushed, the heat rising to her cheeks as she placed her hands on Jack's face. "You love me? You've never told me that before."

Jack nodded. "I thought about it this whole week," he told her as he stared into her dark eyes. "I missed you, Meghan. Even agreeing to take a few days away from you felt…wrong. You are right for me, and I love you."

Jack kissed Meghan gently on the lips, running a hand through her dark hair as she leaned into his embrace. "I love you too, Jack," she murmured.

Jack grinned as he pulled away. "I was hoping you would say that," he admitted. "I am so happy to hear that."

Meghan beamed. "Well, can we celebrate being fully back together and being in love? I have some carrot cake in the back that I know you will love…"

Jack shook his head, and Meghan could see the disappointment in his eyes. "I hate to say it, but I'm actually here on official business."

Meghan raised an eyebrow. "What do you mean?"

Jack shrugged. "There have been some new developments in the investigation of Paula's death. It has officially been ruled a murder, and our lab reports indicate that she died from overdosing on some small tablets. We believe the tablets were slipped into something she ate at the event, and we are talking with every single person who was in the kitchen last night."

Meghan gasped. "But I wasn't in the kitchen! I was a guest. You know that."

Jack agreed. "I do know that, but unfortunately, Trudy and Pamela were not guests. I have been ordered to follow up with everyone, and I was hoping to find them both here."

Meghan sighed. "Pamela is probably at home," she told Jack. "But Trudy...I don't know where Trudy is. She's been acting so out of sorts lately, Jack."

Jack furrowed his brow. "Do you think she had anything to do with Paula's murder?"

Meghan's jaw dropped. "Jack...she's been acting so odd. What if she did? She had access to the ice cream, and I know she takes a variety of medicines for her back. What if Trudy slipped some pills into the ice cream and killed Paula?"

Jack frowned. "It sounds like I need to speak with her immediately, Meghan. I'll send a deputy out to her house to collect her, as well as Pamela."

Meghan nodded. "I'm coming with you," she said. "They are my employees, and if anything happens, I want to be there. I doubt that Pamela had anything to do with Paula's death, but the more we talk about it, the more I think that Trudy knows something."

Jack reached for his coat and fastened the buttons. "Well, I'll call the deputy right now."

Meghan shook her head. "No," she told Jack. "I'll go to Trudy's house. Truly Sweet's reputation would be ruined if she was the one who poisoned Paula, and I want to talk to her *myself*."

11

MEGHAN WALKED QUICKLY up the stone path to Trudy's house. She had never been to Trudy's house before, and she was in awe of the tall, majestic evergreen trees that lined the walkway to Trudy's front door. "I hope this goes well," Meghan thought to herself as she knocked on the front door. "If Trudy had anything to do with Paula's death, I will be *devastated*."

Trudy answered the door after two knocks. "What do you want?" Trudy asked Meghan, her eyes narrowed.

Meghan took a deep breath. "Trudy, you've been acting so strange lately, and I just wanted to check on you. The police have some questions to ask you, and instead of sending a squad car for you, I volunteered to take you to the station. I want to talk with you. I care about you, Trudy, and if you're mixed up in some bad news, I want to help."

Trudy sighed. "Let's go for a walk, shall we?"

Meghan nodded, pleased that Trudy had not slammed the door in her face. The two women took off toward town. Trudy's eyes were cast down at her shoes, and Meghan gently put a hand on Trudy's shoulder. "Trudy, what's wrong?"

Trudy turned away from Meghan. "It's nothing," Trudy griped at Meghan. "I just get sick of you siding with Pamela over me. You're always taking her side, and I'm just left by myself."

Hearing the hurt in Trudy's voice, Meghan tried again. "Trudy," she murmured. "What's going on with you? You haven't been yourself for awhile, and I am concerned."

Trudy began to cry. "I'm sorry," she sputtered as she wiped a tear from her cheek. "You're right. I haven't been myself. It's the anniversary month of my son's passing; he died ten years ago this month, and this time of year is always hard for me."

Meghan reached for Trudy and gathered her in her arms. "Oh, Trudy," Meghan said as she hugged her assistant. "I am so sorry for your loss. I had no idea."

Trudy wiped her nose on her sleeve. "It's fine," she said softly. "I don't tell a lot of people; I don't want to be a burden."

Meghan shook her head. "Trudy," she said. "You're my friend. Your sadness is something I want to know about so I can help."

"Thanks, Meghan," she whispered. "It's just been a difficult month. I'm sorry I've had attitude. I'm sorry

I was rude and taking selfies at the event; my grandson, the son of my late son, got a new phone with a really good camera for me during Thanksgiving, and taking photos has been the only thing taking my mind off of my late son. My grandson asked me to take some photos at the ball; he *adored* Paula Brown's old movies, and he wanted to see if I could snap some pictures of her. I actually have it here, do you want to see?"

Meghan nodded politely, and Trudy showed her several features on the phone. "It captures even the tiniest details. It's been so fun to have something new to try, and I love playing with it. Again, though, Meghan, I am sorry I used it at the ball. I know I shouldn't have."

Meghan smiled. "It's all okay," she told Trudy. "I'm just glad I know that you are okay, Trudy. Let's consider this a fresh start; I'm ready to forget the rough last few weeks if you are?"

Trudy grinned. "Yes, I am," she replied to Meghan. "Being so angry hurts *me*, and I am ready to be back to my normal self."

The two women continued walking. They were on the outskirts of Sandy Bay, and Meghan squinted, recognizing a familiar figure who was walking their way. "Look," Meghan pointed. "It's Pamela. Why don't we say hello?"

The three women greeted each other. "Pamela," Meghan said. "Trudy is ready to start fresh this week.

We can get back to normal at Truly Sweet."

Pamela's face was dark. "I don't know about normal," she responded in a quivering voice. "My mom just called; the police are at my house, and I have to go home. They're looking for me."

Meghan bit her lip. "Yeah, I know," she said. "I was actually going to escort Trudy into the station; Jack told me that the police are talking with everyone who was in the kitchen at the ball, and they want to interview the pair of you. It shouldn't be too difficult, though; as long as you answer their questions honestly, it will all be okay. They'll probably ask about your whereabouts before the ball, your feelings toward Paula, and some other questions about the night she died."

As the trio arrived at the police station, Meghan's stomach churned when she spotted the reporter in the trench coat who had shown up at the bakery. He waved at her, smiling wolfishly as he shoved a microphone in her face.

"Meghan Truman, can you say a few words on the investigation of Paula Brown's death? Is there a reason you are accompanying two of the police's suspects to the station?"

Meghan glared at the reporter. "You should have told me you were a reporter when you asked me questions in my bakery," she hissed.

The reporter smirked. "You should have been smart

enough to figure that out."

Meghan gritted her teeth as she tried to push past the reporter. "Get out of our way. We are trying to get inside of the station, and you are blocking us from entering."

The reporter chuckled. "I'm not moving until you answer my questions. Now, Meghan, what can you tell us about Paula Brown's murder? I hear the police have declared her death to be a murder. Can you say more on the state of the investigation?"

Meghan's face was burning with anger, and as the reporter jabbed the microphone back into her face, Meghan tore it from his hands. She reared back, and sent the microphone crashing down on the concrete steps of the police station.

"Hey! You cannot do that," the reporter exclaimed as he bent down to collect the pieces of his broken microphone. "I'll sue you for that. That's my private property, and you ruined it."

Just as Meghan opened her mouth to argue, a police officer walked out of the station. "Officer," the reporter pleaded. "This woman damaged my property. I would like to file a police report immediately."

The police officer looked between Meghan and the reporter, and then down at the pieces of the microphone that lay on the ground. "I didn't see anything," the officer replied, slicking back his hair and nodding kindly at Meghan. "Besides, I know Ms.

Truman here would never hurt a fly, let along damage the property of a slimeball reporter like yourself."

The reporter frowned. "Excuse me?"

The officer narrowed his eyes. "That report you did on the local schools? It was demeaning for teachers; you suggested that Sandy Bay teachers don't care about their students. Guess what, buddy? My wife is a teacher, and you hurt her feelings with that trashy piece of journalism. My word here is that Meghan didn't touch you, or your microphone. Now, you all have a good day."

The officer strutted away, and Meghan flipped her hair behind her shoulder. "You heard him," she gloated to the reporter. "You have a good day."

As Meghan turned on her heel and marched into the station, Pamela turned to Trudy and whispered, in awe "I've learned something today, Trudy: no one messes with Meghan Truman. She may be truly *sweet*, but she is also truly *fierce*."

12

THE POLICE STATION WAS BUSTLING; Meghan saw dozens of people waiting to be interviewed, and the three women could not find a free chair amongst the crowd.

"Hey, those people were working in the kitchen with us," Pamela whispered to Meghan as she pointed to four mustached men. "They were part of Claude's team. There was another guy with them who was my age, and man, he was so cute."

Meghan laughed. "Pamela, you silly goose."

The three women sat down on the floor of the station. Suddenly, Jack emerged from his office, and Meghan perked up, shyly tucking her hair behind her ears and straightening her posture.

"With that look in your eyes, I'm going to guess that things are fine with you and Jack?" Trudy asked as she leaned against the wall.

"Yes," Meghan confirmed with a huge smile on her face. "We talked it all through, and it's all going to be okay."

Trudy grinned. "I'm so happy to hear that."

Jack approached the women, and Meghan stood up to plant a kiss on his cheek. Jack smiled sheepishly, and then, he gave Meghan a sweet kiss on the lips.

"Gross!" Pamela screeched as Trudy shushed her.

"That's how I know you aren't ready for a French boyfriend," Meghan laughed.

Jack's face turned serious as he surveyed the busy hallway. "We have over a hundred people to interview," he whispered into Meghan's ear. "We reviewed some of the footage from the kitchen tapes, and we are likely still going to speak with Trudy and Pamela. Chief Nunan asked me to keep everyone corralled here, though, so if you could just stay a bit longer?"

Meghan nodded. "No problem. We'll keep ourselves entertained, right, ladies?"

Trudy smiled. "We can play around with my new phone camera. Pamela, I was showing Meghan my new toy earlier, but now I can show you. I have some cute pictures of you from the Governor's Ball. Do you want to see?"

Pamela grinned. "Yes! Cute candid pictures are my favorite; I want to post some online if they're super cute."

Jack kissed Meghan's forehead and walked back to

his office. The three women settled back on the floor. Trudy removed her phone from her coat and began scrolling through her photos.

"This is a picture of you, Pamela," Trudy said as she showed Pamela the screen. "Look how cute you look in your Truly Sweet smock. Just adorable."

Meghan gestured at the screen. "I knew you both would look gorgeous in the smocks. What other photos do you have on there, Trudy? Any photos of me?"

"Well, you weren't in the kitchen, so probably not, but let me check," Trudy told Meghan. "There are some videos on here. Meghan, why don't you look? My eyes are starting to hurt some squinting at this tiny screen."

Trudy handed the phone to Meghan, and she began to thumb through the videos and images. She stopped when she saw a familiar face, smiling as she recalled her pleasant encounter with the subject.

"This is Donnie," Meghan exclaimed as she tilted the phone toward Pamela and Trudy. "He was Paula's assistant. I met him in the fruit market, and he was so kind. He wants to get into politics someday. We had a great chat. I bet he would like some of these candid photos. He looks so elegant in his outfit!"

Meghan flipped through several more candid shots of Donnie. "Ooooh, there's a video, too," Meghan told the women. "Oh no…."

After pressing play, Meghan's heart began to pound. On the small screen of the camera, Meghan watched as Donnie reached into his pocket and retrieved something that looked like tablets. Meghan scrolled to the next video, where she saw Donnie look right, and then left, and then drop the tablets into a bowl of ice cream.

"Oh my goodness," Meghan whispered as she froze the image. "It was Donnie. Donnie poisoned Paula. Her own assistant poisoned her!"

Trudy grabbed the camera from Meghan and stared at the tiny video screen. "Let me see that," Trudy ordered.

"You're right," Trudy concluded, her eyes widening as the second video ended. "He did it. That man in my video poisoned the ice cream, and we have video evidence. Meghan, you need to take my camera to your sweetheart right now!"
Meghan stood up from her place on the floor. She sprinted down the hallway and burst into Jack's office. "Jack, I know who poisoned Paula. You can send all of these people home; Donnie, Paula's assistant, killed her, and I have video evidence."

"Is that so?"

Meghan nodded as Chief Nunan stepped into the room. "I heard what you said, Meghan," Chief Nunan told her. "Is the video on that phone?"

Meghan bobbed her head and gave the phone to Chief

Nunan. "It's all on there, Chief Nunan. See for
yourself."

Chief Nunan turned on the camera and watched the
two videos. "Yes, you are right," Chief Nunan said as
the second video ended. "We have enough evidence
to arrest Donnie, Paula's assistant. Jack? I want you
to spread the word: Donnie is now our primary
suspect, and I have great reason to believe that he
killed his employer. I want every officer and detective
out on this guy, and I want him brought to me
immediately."

13

"ALL OF THIS HAPPENED while I was on my yoga retreat?" Karen Denton laughed into the phone as Meghan strolled down the beach. "To think I missed the ball, a breakup, and a murder! I moved back to Sandy Bay for some peace and quiet, but it feels like peace and quiet is never quite the case…"

Meghan chuckled, happy to hear her dear friend's voice. Karen had been in Costa Rica for nearly two weeks, and Meghan could hardly wait to fill her in on all of the events following the Governor's Ball.

"This is why you had to go find inner peace," Meghan joked. "You knew you couldn't find it here, so you had to go all the way to Costa Rica."

Karen giggled. "You caught me. Speaking of getting caught…tell me about how they caught that Donnie ding-dong. I can't believe he killed his own boss."

"I know," she agreed. "It's terrible. Jack and Chief Nunan dragged Donnie kicking and screaming out of the Governor's Mansion about an hour after I showed them the video. They found more poison in the

Governor's kitchen, and it looks like Donnie was
planning to kill the Governor, too."
"Good thing Trudy showed you that footage, or other
innocent people would have died," Karen said.
"Seriously, I just can't believe she caught it on film
by accident. What are the odds?"

Meghan shivered as a gust of cold wind slapped her
face. She zipped her long, purple coat higher up her
neck and shuddered; she hated being cold, and despite
loving her life in Sandy Bay, when it was chilly,
Meghan ached for the mild Los Angeles weather that
she had previously lived in.

"So did Jack tell you why Donnie did it?" Karen
asked.

"Donnie confessed right away. He told Jack and
Chief Nunan that Paula had undermined his political
aspirations by reporting him to the Governor's
compliance officer for not declaring a gift he had
received while on official duty, and had threatened
that she was going to ruin his chances at being elected
to office someday."

Karen sighed. "I hope that buffoon knows now that
he'll never be elected; he not only killed his boss, but
he ruined his own life."

"He did," Meghan said. "He ruined his life, but
thankfully, mine is back on track; Jack and I had
dinner with his friend, Michelle, and I was able to
apologize for being rude, and she even apologized for
not thinking of my feelings. She and I probably won't

ever be best friends, but at least we aren't enemies."

"That's good," Karen agreed. "It's never good to have an enemy. So…Jack? What's going on there? Are things okay?"

Despite the harsh winds biting at her skin, Meghan beamed. "We're okay, Karen. Actually, we are more than okay; when Jack and I were making up, he told me that he loves me. I said it back to him, too. We are in love, and better than ever."

"That's wonderful news," Karen cooed as Meghan thought about her handsome boyfriend. "I'm over the moon that things have worked out. I wish I could have been in Sandy Bay to help you, but it sounds like you were able to fix things yourself."

Meghan grinned, thinking of how happy she was that she and Jack were back together, and imagining how she had stood up to the reporter outside of the police station. Meghan's heart warmed as she remembered the shy, meek girl she had been when she arrived in Sandy Bay, and compared that girl to the strong, resilient woman she was now.

"I've been learning to stand up for myself, Karen," Meghan informed her friend. "I feel like I learn something new every single day here in Sandy Bay. Even the bad days have given me valuable lessons, and I can honestly say, without hesitation, that no matter the challenges, it is truly sweet to be in Sandy Bay with all of my friends and my *loved* ones!"

The End

Afterword

Thank you for reading Ice Cream and Guilty Pleasures! I really hope you enjoyed reading it as much as I had writing it!

If you have a minute, please consider leaving a review on Amazon, GoodReads and/or Bookbub.

Many thanks in advance for your support!

About Jingle Bells and Deadly Smells

Released: December 2018
Series: Book 10 – Sandy Bay Cozy Mystery Series
Standalone: Yes
Cliff-hanger: No

Christmas is that season…that season of pleasant surprises…delicious smells…and family and friends to share the holidays with.

This Christmas, Sandy Bay's lovable bakery owner, Meghan Truman, gets a whole lot more than she bargained for…plus a dead body at the door of her favorite restaurant. Some people would rather sweep this murder under the carpet but something smells awfully fishy about the events surrounding it.

Will Meghan join Detective Irvin to find the murderer or will this event serve to etch unpleasant memories of this most wonderful time of the year?

JINGLE BELLS AND DEADLY SMELLS CHAPTER 1 SNEEK PEEK

IT WAS GOING TO BE A WHITE CHRISTMAS in Sandy Bay, and Meghan Truman could hardly contain her excitement as the glittering white snowflakes tumbled from the sky. Meghan shivered as she adjusted the pink tartan scarf around her neck, thankful for its comfort as she stepped outside into the chilly evening. Meghan set off down the street toward Spark, a new boutique in town. She was ten minutes late for her shopping date with Jackie, her close friend, and Meghan trudged through the snow in her knee-length brown boots.

"Can you spare a dime, Miss?"

Meghan bit her bottom lip as a homeless man on the corner beckoned her toward him. She nervously ran a hand through her long, dark hair, shaking her head as she passed.

"I'm sorry," Meghan muttered as she looked down at her boots. "I don't have any cash."

Her heart sank as she walked away from the homeless man, and her cheeks burned with shame. She truly did not have any cash on her, but Meghan's chest tightened with guilt as she considered the man's plight. "Perhaps I could have given him my gloves," she thought to herself. "Or I could have dashed home and fetched some treats for him from the bakery."

She was the sole owner of Truly Sweet, a wildly successful bakery in Sandy Bay. She had opened the bakery after moving to Sandy Bay from Los Angeles less than a year ago, and now, after months of persistence and perseverance, Truly Sweet was one of the most popular bakeries in the Pacific Northwest. Meghan's orders had more than quadrupled in the last three months, and she was thankful for the help of Trudy, her assistant, and Pamela, the high-school girl she had hired to help with the heavy workload.

"I have so much stale bread and old pastries sitting in my pantry," she murmured, still distraught by her interaction with the homeless man. "It is so cold tonight, and he needs to eat. I will just have to be a few more minutes late to my shopping date."

Meghan turned around, treading back through the heavy snow. She unlocked the front door of the bakery, smiling as the familiar sound of the little silver bells attached to the door jingled merrily. She heard her little twin dogs barking upstairs in her apartment, but she ignored them, sprinting into the kitchen of the bakery and removing a bag of old pastries and breads from the closet.

"Perfect," Meghan said, satisfied as she filled a cloth sack with the food. "I can drop these off with that man, and hopefully, he will go to bed with a full belly tonight."

She raced out of the bakery and back onto the slippery streets. She nearly fell as her feet slipped beneath her, but she regained her composure and marched off toward the corner where she had encountered the homeless man.

"Oh no," Meghan sighed as she arrived to find the man had vanished. "He's gone. I was too late."

She hung her head, wishing she had had something to give the man when she first met him. "Maybe I'll see him again someday," Meghan considered as she rested the bag of food down on the side of street. "Maybe he'll come back. I'll leave this food here for now. I hope he finds it."

Jackie chastised Meghan as she entered the shop. "Where have you been? You are too late, girlfriend. This is the second time this week you've been late to a hang out."

Meghan's cheeks burned, and she sheepishly apologized to Jackie, explaining why she was late.

"Oh, Meghan," Jackie said kindly as she saw the tears in her dark eyes. "You were full of the holiday spirit. I'm proud of you. What a good person you are."

Meghan shrugged. "I just think everyone deserves a

full belly and a warm bed."

Jackie smiled. "Your heart is truly sweet, Meghan. Hey, speaking of Truly Sweet, are you doing the desserts for Jack's holiday party?"

Meghan grinned at the mention of Jack Irvin, her handsome detective boyfriend. "No," she explained to Jackie. "Chief Nunan reached out and asked me to do the desserts, but I decided to pass the chance up; I want to go to the party as a guest, and I think dealing with the desserts would be a lot of stress."

Jackie nodded. "That makes sense," she told Meghan. "Well, the Sandy Bay Police Department Christmas Party is always a huge event in town. Everyone dresses up, and there is mistletoe, and it's just magical."

Meghan smiled. "I need to find the perfect dress; do you think I would look nice in red velvet?"

Jackie squinted her eyes at Meghan, looking up and down at her curvy frame. "Yes," she finally replied. "I think with your dark hair and olive skin, you would glow in red velvet. Come on! Let's see what this shop has to offer."

"Ladies!"

Meghan and Jackie turned to find Kirsty Fisher beaming at them, her blonde bob sitting elegantly just above her shoulders, and a strand of tiny pearls wrapped around her thin neck. Kirsty was a dedicated philanthropist and organizer in the community; if there was an event or party, it was likely that Kirsty had planned and put on the event, and she was always looking for favors as she dreamed up new functions for the town.

"So good to see you girls," Kirsty cooed as she gave Meghan and Jackie air-kisses on both cheeks. "In fact, I was just thinking of you, Meghan. What are you doing next weekend?"

Meghan grimaced. "Why do you ask, Kirsty?"

Kirsty adjusted her red and green sweater set and smiled warmly. "I'm organizing a celebration of Christmas carols, and I would love if you could help me."

Meghan paused. She had intentionally slowed her schedule over the last week, and she was looking forward to some much-needed rest and recuperation after such a busy, eventful year in Sandy Bay.

"Kirsty," Meghan began. "I'm not really taking on new orders right now; I'm not even doing the desserts for Jack's holiday party. It's been a hectic year, and I am trying to give myself, along with Trudy and Pamela, some time to catch our breath."

Kirsty shook her head. "I don't want your treats," she informed her. "I need your voice. I am trying to recruit anyone and everyone to participate, and for a small donation, you can join in the fun."

Meghan raised an eyebrow. "I have a terrible voice," she told Kirsty. "It's horrendous; I was actually cut from my middle-school choir because I am tone-deaf."

Kirsty waved her hands dismissively. "You can just lip-sync, then. Jackie, I'm sure you can sing on pitch. Would you join us?"

Jackie wrinkled her nose. "My voice isn't good…"

Kirsty huffed in frustration. "This is for a good cause, girls," she informed Meghan and Jackie. "The donations are being given to the local homeless agency, and with the holidays just around the corner, it is important to think of others."

The image of the homeless man on the corner from earlier flashed through Meghan's mind, and she nodded emphatically. "Yes, you are right," she said to Kirsty. "We'll both be there."

Kirsty tossed her blonde hair behind her shoulder and smiled haughtily. "That's what I wanted to hear," she told both ladies. "Wonderful. Just bring something for the homeless folks who attend. You can even bring something store-bought, Meghan. Just make sure you have something for them, as well as your donation. Toodles, girls! See you at the Christmas carol."

Jackie rolled her eyes as Kirsty sashayed out of the boutique. "How did we just get roped into that?"

Meghan shrugged. "Kirsty is right," she told Jackie. "It's the season of love and giving. I can whip up a batch of cookies to take with me, and we'll both go. Besides, it's only for a few hours, and it's for a great cause. What could go wrong?

On the evening of the event, Jack picked Meghan up from the bakery. His blonde hair was smoothed down with gel, and Meghan thought he looked handsome in his green Christmas sweater.

"Thanks for going with me tonight," Meghan said to Jack as she leaned up on her tiptoes to kiss him softly on the lips.

"Of course," he replied. "It's a good cause, and I'm proud of you."

Meghan smiled. "It will be fun. It's always good to give back."

Jack and Meghan drove to the Sandy Bay Community Center, and as he helped Meghan out of the car, her eyes sparkled with joy. "Look at the decorations," she cried, pointing to a ten-foot high Christmas tree positioned outside of the main entry. "It's beautiful."

Jack playfully swatted Meghan on the arm. "Don't you know by now that Sandy Bay knows how to celebrate?"

Jack took Meghan's hand as they entered the massive main room. Meghan saw Kirsty assembling carolers onto bleachers, and she waved at Jackie from across the room. "I'm going to go get settled. Can you put my cookies on that dessert table over there?"

Jack nodded, taking the bag from Meghan's hands. "Of course. You go have fun!"

Meghan scurried over to where the singers were corralled, but as she began to ascend the stairs to her row on the bleachers, she heard a shout. Meghan turned to see four men shoving each other next to the dessert table.

"I want all of those cookies. You ate too much cake."

"Don't be selfish. My kids need some food too."

"This stupid party was the only way to get some good food, and I'm going to take what I want."

Meghan saw one of the men reach into the bag and take out her cookies. From his tattered clothes and greasy hair, she presumed he was homeless. She watched in horror as he threw her cookies onto the floor.

"I'll be right back," Meghan whispered to Jackie as she took off across the room. "Hey, sir? Sir? I only made enough so that each person could have two cookies."

The man scowled, but he nodded at Meghan. "Sorry. I was just excited."

Meghan felt a hard tap on her shoulder. She heard Jack's deep voice coming toward her. "Don't you touch her!"

Meghan's heart beat faster as she turned around. Jack ran to her side, but as she made eye contact with the man who touched her shoulder, she gasped.

"What do you think you are doing?" Jack demanded as he stepped between Meghan and the man. "Keep your hands off of my girlfriend."

The man chuckled, winking at Meghan. "Who do I think I am? Meghan, honey? Wanna tell 'em?"

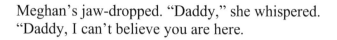

Meghan's jaw-dropped. "Daddy," she whispered. "Daddy, I can't believe you are here.

-

You can order your copy of **Jingle Bells and Deadly Smells** at any good online retailer.

ALSO BY AMBER CREWES

The Sandy Bay Cozy Mystery Series

Apple Pie and Trouble

Brownies and Dark Shadows

Cookies and Buried Secrets

Donuts and Disaster

Éclairs and Lethal Layers

Finger Foods and Missing Legs

Gingerbread and Scary Endings

Hot Chocolate and Cold Bodies

Ice Cream and Guilty Pleasures

Jingle Bells and Deadly Smells

King Cake and Grave Mistakes

Lemon Tarts and Fiery Darts

Muffins and Coffins

Nuts and a Choking Corpse

Orange Mousse and a Fatal Truce

Newsletter Signup

Want **FREE** COPIES OF FUTURE **AMBER CREWES** BOOKS, FIRST NOTIFICATION OF NEW RELEASES, CONTESTS AND GIVEAWAYS?

GO TO THE LINK BELOW TO SIGN UP TO THE NEWSLETTER!

www.AmberCrewes.com/cozylist

Manufactured by Amazon.ca
Bolton, ON